Zippy Schnauzers in France

Mica Jorgensen
Illustrated by Maria Andrieieva

Published by Coucou Publications

ISBN: 978-0-6488402-0-6 (ebook)
ISBN: 978-0-6488402-1-3 (paperback)
ISBN: 978-0-6488402-2-0 (hardback)

To all the wonderful bakers in the world

"Kaiser, Otto—we are going on an adventure around France," say Mama and Papa.

We continue to nap, comfortable in our beds.

"Are you lazy boys? Come on, there will be crunchy baguettes everywhere!"

We jump up.

"When do we leave?" we ask.

But Mama and Papa do not tell us it is not easy getting our paws on the baguettes.

Sniff, sniff!

We spot the first baguette, do you?

But, oh no, there are more than a thousand steps to the top.

It will take all day to reach up there.

If only we were not so lazy.

We continue on our trip.

Sniff, sniff!

We spot another baguette, do you?

But, oh no, there are bees surrounding the baguette.

We are getting hungry but we are afraid to get stung.

Oh la la! We spot yet another baguette, do you?

But, oh no, it is high tide and we have to swim to the island to get to the baguette.

The smell of the crunchy baguette spreads across the bay and makes us hungrier.

What can we do?
Schnauzers do not like
to get wet.

This time we decide to ask for help.

"Monsieur Labrador, since you like to swim,
would you mind if we get a ride on your back?"

"Sure, but we Labradors like to eat too, so you'll have to share the baguette."

SPLASH SPLASH

One baguette for three hungry dogs is just not enough. We are still hungry.

We continue our trip and head for the mountains.

Soon we see a group of cyclists.

Wait, we spot a baguette, do you?

But, oh no, the cyclist with the baguette is too fast!

What can we do?

Aha—let's work together!

The two of us can be twice as fast.

ZOOM!

We grab the baguette, but all that huffing and puffing on the bike makes us hungrier.

We need more baguettes.

Further along, we
stop to admire the
rows and rows
of grapes but it's
a baguette that
catches our eyes.

But, oh, why is the man holding the baguette stomping on grapes?

Is he working or having fun? Maybe both!

Let's dance
to the squish
of the grapes
while we get
closer to the
baguette!

Tappity tap tap

A skip

A twist for a baguette stick

We then giggle and jiggle our way to a castle.

Look! We spot a baguette up high, do you?

Every day the best baguettes
are sent to the king who
lives there.

Who does not want to
taste the best baguette?

But, oh no, the castle has a
big fortress wall.

We ask the knight
politely to let us in,
but unlike the helpful
Monsieur Labrador,
the knight yells a loud,
"NO!"

Our stomachs rumble so loud from hunger, we cannot sneak past the knight without him hearing us.

Since we cannot go past the knight, let's try another way.

Aha-let's aim high!

The king hears the stories of our zippy adventures all around France and invites us to stay in the castle.

"How brave you are to go after what you love!" the king praises.

The king then presents to us with a whole basket of today's best baguettes.

Our stomachs let out a growl
of excitement.

After many baguette adventures across the country, we return home.

"Kaiser, Otto—do you want more baguette?" ask Mama and Papa.

We never refuse an offering of baguette.

"Sit and roll over," they say.

The two of us look at each other and smile.

We now know there is a better, fun way to get the baguette.

Licks and kisses for
Mama and Papa!

If you enjoy the book, please sign up at www.zippyschnauzers.com for updates and leave a review at your retailer. Reviews for this book can bring to the attention of other readers who may enjoy it.
Find us also on Instagram and Facebook @zippyschnauzers

Printed in Great Britain
by Amazon